THIS LITTLE TIGER BOOK BELONGS TO:

_____

_____

_____

_____

for
Alice Elizabeth

LITTLE TIGER PRESS
1 The Coda Centre, 189 Munster Road
London SW6 6AW

This paperback edition published 1999
First published in Great Britain 1999

Text and illustrations © 1999 Catherine Walters

Printed in Belgium by Proost NV, Turnhout

ISBN 1 85430 618 9

3 5 7 9 10 8 6 4

Are you there, Baby Bear?

CATHERINE WALTERS

LITTLE TIGER PRESS
London

"Play with me, Mum," said Alfie.
"Not now," replied his mother. "I'm tired."
"And I'm bored," wailed Alfie. "I've got
nothing to do."
"You'll have plenty to do soon,"
promised Mother Bear, "when your
new brother or sister arrives."

A new brother or sister!
Alfie couldn't wait.

Every morning he asked Mother Bear,
"Is my new brother coming today?"

And every evening at bedtime he said,
"Will my sister come tonight?"

"The new baby will come when it's ready," promised Mother Bear.

The weather grew colder and it was nearly time for the bears' winter sleep, but still the baby bear had not arrived.
"It might be lost," worried Alfie. "Perhaps it can't find its way in the snow."

So one morning, very early, Alfie crept out of the cave to go looking for his baby brother or sister.

Alfie walked to the edge of the frozen lake,
where the ducks were waddling in the reeds.
And there, where the sun was melting the ice,
Alfie saw – *a baby bear!*
"Are you my new brother?" he called out.

"Sorry, little bear, I'm not your new brother,"
said Beaver, slapping her tail. "I'll look
out for him, though, and send
him home if I see him."
Alfie thanked her. "Perhaps the new
baby's in the meadow," he thought.

In the meadow the mountain hares
bounded across Alfie's path.
And there, through the frozen bracken,
Alfie saw – *a baby bear!*
"Are you my new sister?" he shouted.

"Certainly not!" snorted Bison, standing up and
shaking himself. "I'm afraid she's not your little
sister. She's mine!"
Bison's sister sniffed Alfie all over. "We'll let
you know if we see any bears," she said.
"Thank you," said Alfie. "I think I'll
go and look in the woods."

In the woods the squirrels leapt and
chased each other through the trees.
And, stretched along a tree branch,
Alfie saw – *a baby bear!*
"Are you our new baby?" he yelled.

"Certainly not!" yawned Mountain Lion,
staring down at Alfie's worried face.
"But as you've woken me up I'll watch out
for baby bears if you like."
Alfie sighed. He was beginning to wonder
if he'd *ever* find Baby Bear!

Alfie plodded on. He saw wolves and deer and
sleepy brown owls, but no baby bears.
He was a long way from home and he was cold
and tired. Just as he was wondering what to do
next, Alfie saw Father Bear coming towards him.
"There you are, Alfie," cried Father Bear.
"We've been looking for you all day."
And, very gently, he picked Alfie up
and carried him all the way home.

Mother Bear was waiting for them by the cave.
"I've been out looking for our baby," Alfie told her.
"But there were no baby bears *anywhere.*"
"Oh Alfie," said Mother Bear, cuddling him close.
"You didn't look here, did you?"

Alfie peered into the darkness of the cave and his
eyes grew round. "Is it a baby brother or a sister?"
he whispered. Mother Bear took his paw and
they all crept inside.

"BOTH!"
she said.

Join the LITTLE TIGER CLUB now and receive a special Little Tiger goody bag containing badges, pencils and more! Once you become a member you will be sent details of special offers, competitions and news of new books. Why not write a book review? The best reviews will be published on book covers or in the Little Tiger Press catalogue.

The LITTLE TIGER CLUB is free to join. Members can cancel their membership at any time, and are under no obligation to purchase any books. If you would like details of the Little Tiger Club, please contact: Little Tiger Press 1 The Coda Centre, 189 Munster Road, London SW6 6AW, UK Telephone: 020 7385 6333 Fax: 020 7385 7333 E-Mail: info@littletiger.co.uk